MY FRIENDS
MAX LOW

Otter-Barry BOOKS

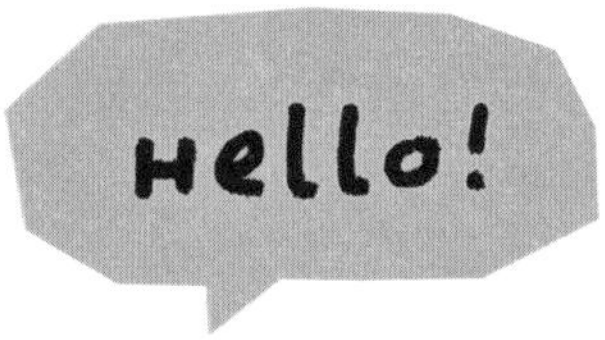
Hello!

I've made some friends. Would you like to meet them?

Mossy is a good friend
to be quiet with.

shhh

We don't always have to talk. Sometimes we just sit and dream together.

Archibald
likes lions.
He makes a
good lion.

Raaa

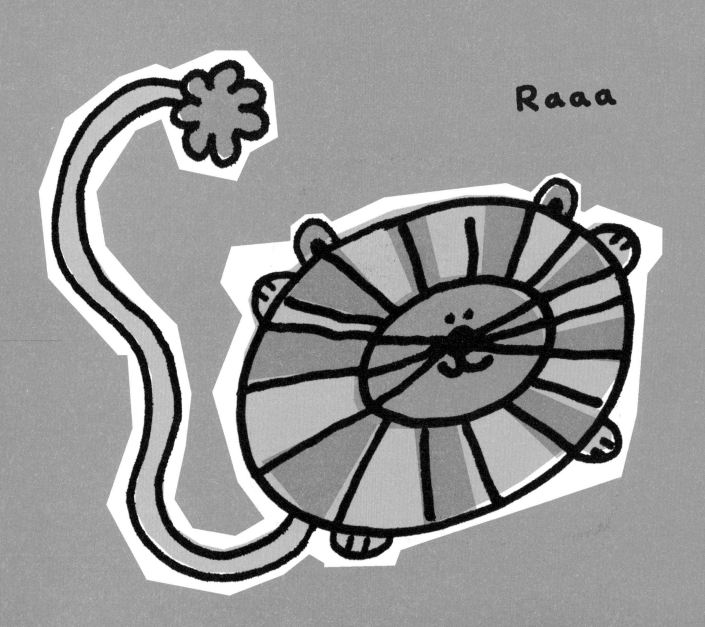

Top 5 animals
1-Lions
2-lions
3-lions
4-lions
5-lions

I could watch clouds
all day with Ezza.

This one is a big beard to keep a chin warm.

Look at that one. It's a woolly mammoth!

That one is a poodle!

Pepper cooks
me yummy food.

I wash up.

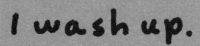

Olga is the friend
I like to listen to
music with.

we drink hot squash
while we listen.

Herman has
an interest
in knitting.

So far he has
made a tangle.
We are all
very proud.

Lina
invents
things.

I invented something
once, but Lina had
already invented it.
She's good at that.

Bert
looks
after
worms
and
flies
and
slugs
and
snails.

He takes care of them
because he is big
and they are small.

This is Plim.

Plim likes to pretend to phone people. He mostly talks about the weather.

This is Klaus,
my imaginary friend.

It's good to have an
imaginary friend
because they can
be with you whenever
you need them.

I love my friends.

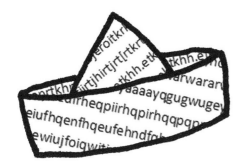

But sometimes...

NICE
THINGS

I just like to
be by myself.